THE ADVENTURES OF
THOR
THE THUNDER GOD

RETOLD BY LISE LUNGE-LARSEN

ILLUSTRATED BY JIM MADSEN

HOUGHTON MIFFLIN COMPANY

BOSTON 2007

To Ian and Torstein
– L.L.-L.

For my three children:
Mckenzie, Hannah, and Easton
– J.M.

www.houghtonmifflinbooks.com

The text of this book is set in Trump Mediaeval.
The illustrations are digital.

Library of Congress Cataloging-in-Publication Data
Lunge-Larsen, Lise.
The adventures of Thor the Thunder God / retold by Lise Lunge-Larsen ;
illustrated by Jim Madsen
p. cm.
ISBN 0-618-47301-7
1. Thor (Norse deity) — Juvenile literature.
I. Madsen, Jim, 1964– II. Title.
BL870.T5L86 2007
398.2'0948'01 — dc22
2004015765

ISBN-13: 978-0-618-47301-4

Printed in Singapore

TWP 10 9 8 7 6 5 4 3 2 1

Contents

Why Thor is Called the Thunder God

*Long, long ago, when the Vikings ruled the seas,
people loved to tell stories about gods and giants.
Renowned as warriors and sailors, the Vikings were
also great storytellers. Their most treasured stories
were about a god named Thor.*

The Vikings worshiped many gods, but Thor was their favorite because he was the biggest, strongest, and bravest. He kept everyone safe from the evil giants. From the beginning of time, the gods and the giants disliked each other. The giants, who were huge and ugly, were jealous of the gods' beauty. They also hated the gods for being cleverer than they were. You see, the giants knew some magic, but not magic so deep that living things sprang from it. Only the gods knew that kind of magic, and with it they had created the world and all the beings that lived there.

More than anything, the giants wanted to destroy the earth, or Midgard as the Vikings called it. They wanted to destroy the gods' favorite creation, human beings. But as long as Thor protected them, this could not be. No wonder the Vikings loved him best.

Because Thor was so important to them, many Vikings carved his likeness into the central pillars of their homes and even gave his name to one of the days of the week: Thursday, which means Thor's Day.

Their stories told how Thor loved to fight giants. To help overcome them, he had a special belt that doubled his strength! The best weapon in fighting giants, however, was Thor's hammer. It was named Mjolnir the Thunderbolt and the giants feared it above all else, for it had crushed many of their skulls. The Vikings had so much confidence in Thor's hammer that they often carried a small model of it for good luck and protection.

Thor usually traveled about in his carriage, which was pulled by Toothgnasher and Toothgrinder, two goats that ground their teeth so fiercely that sparks flew. When they raced across the sky with Thor, their hooves kicked up huge thunderclouds down in Midgard, where humans lived, and Thor's hammer made lightning flash. When they heard the big boom of thunder, people in Midgard rejoiced because this meant the hammer had hit its target and Thor had protected them. That's why they called him "Thor, the Thunder God."

The Giants

In the Vikings' stories, there were two kinds of giants: trolls and jotuns. All giants lived in a mountainous land called Jotunheim at the very eastern edge of Midgard.

The trolls were enormously strong, but they were also very stupid and could not stay out when the sun was shining. If they did, they would burst and turn into stone. The jotuns, however, were a much bigger problem for the gods. They were just as big and nasty as the trolls but far more cunning. They had heads of stone and feet of ice and they could be out when the sun was shining. But that was not all! They could also change shape and play magic tricks that fooled even the gods.

One strange thing about jotuns was that even though they were big and mean, they sometimes had beautiful, kindhearted daughters. So lovely were these maidens that once in a while a god would fall in love with one and marry her. In fact, Thor's mother was such a jotun maiden. It is possible that Thor inherited his enormous strength from her.

Thor's Family

Thor and the other gods lived in Asgard, the citadel of the gods located high above Midgard but connected to it by a rainbow bridge. Thirteen mighty halls surrounded the citadel, and Thor's hall was the biggest. It had 540 rooms, which he shared with his wife and children.

Thor's father, Odin, was the chief of all the gods. He once sacrificed one of his eyes to be allowed to drink out of the Well of Wisdom and so became the wisest among all living things.

Before he gained his great wisdom, when he was still quite young, Odin became friends with a jotun named Loki. Unlike other jotuns, Loki was graceful and handsome, and he was smaller than most giants, about the size of Odin. He was quick-witted and full of clever ideas and tricks. Odin and Loki became foster brothers, and in this way Loki became one of the gods and went to live in Asgard — for better and for worse.

Loki's Bet

Thor had a fierce temper and fiery red hair and a beard to match. But his wife, Sif, had hair more beautiful than anyone had ever seen. It gleamed and shimmered like golden wheat. One morning when Thor woke up, a terrible sight met his eyes. In the night, someone had cut off Sif's hair. Not one of her lovely tresses was left. And you have to understand, unlike human hair, Sif's hair would never grow out again.

The only one in Asgard who would do such a mean-spirited and shameful thing was Loki.

"I'm going to break every bone in his body," roared Thor, storming off in such a rage that sparks flew. He searched everywhere till he found Loki trembling inside a cupboard, for he was guilty indeed.

"Help! Spare me! I'm sorry," begged Loki. "I will bring Sif new hair. I can make the dwarfs forge hair of solid gold if only you will spare me."

Thor would have liked to crush him, but he knew Loki was the only one clever enough to undo his own mischief. So for the love of his wife, Thor let Loki go.

Off went Loki, through the mountains of Midgard, to Svartheim, where the dwarfs dwelled. There he sought out two dwarfs called the sons of Ivald. Usually dwarfs refuse to do favors for anyone, but Loki knew just how to flatter them.

"Oh! What exquisite work you do. You must be the best smiths in the world," he said. Looking downcast, he added, "I need a blacksmith, but I'm afraid the task is too difficult even for you."

"What is it?" grunted the dwarfs. "We have never yet come up against a job too difficult for our skill."

"It is to make new hair for Sif," said Loki.

Without a word the dwarfs went to their forge and threw a bar of gold into the fire. They worked the gold with their tiny hammers, beating and chanting until they had beaten the gold into threads as fine as silk. The strands shimmered with a thousand lights.

Loki was pleased, but he was still nervous about facing Thor.

"Amazing! Just wait till the gods see this. Surely you'll never make anything finer," he said.

Wanting to impress the gods, the sons of Ivald made two more treasures: a ship that could sail in the air as well as on the sea and a spear that would hit its mark no matter how poor the aim.

Loki clapped his hands in delight and brought the gifts back to Asgard. When he placed the golden hair on Sif's head, it attached itself as though it had roots and fell down over her shoulders and back like a cascading river of finely spun gold. All the gods and goddesses laughed with happiness to see Sif's beautiful hair restored.

Then Loki brought out the other two treasures, and the gods, even Thor, forgave him instantly. Ah, but now Loki became so proud of how cleverly he had saved himself that he started boasting.

"My friends are the best blacksmiths in all of Svartheim. I bet no other dwarf can make treasures as great as these."

"Don't you be so sure," shrieked a tiny dwarf trembling with rage. It was Brokk, who was visiting Asgard. "My brother Sindri is the best smith in all of Svartheim. Everybody knows it. The work by your friends is pitiful compared with my brother's work."

"No, it isn't!" shouted Loki. "I'll bet my head against yours that nothing your brother makes is as good as what my friends have made today."

"We'll see about that!" shouted Brokk. "And when I bring the treasures back, the gods will judge whose work is best." With that, he rushed off.

"Don't worry," said Sindri when Brokk arrived at his smithy in Svartheim. "You shall not lose your head. I am indeed the best smith in the world and I can prove it as long as you keep the fire steady."

Throwing a pig's skin into the fire, Sindri said, "Now keep the bellows going, and no matter what, don't stop until I tell you."

Brokk kept the fire blazing by moving the bellows steadily in and out. All at once a stinging fly came into the smithy. It buzzed around Brokk, then sat down on his hand and bit. Brokk roared with pain but he did not let go of the bellows, for he realized the fly must be Loki, who, like all jotuns, could change his shape.

Gritting his teeth, Brokk continued pumping. When Sindri finished, he pulled out a boar, big enough to ride, with golden bristles that glimmered and shone like the sun itself. This boar could race in the air, and never would the night be so dark, even in the underworld, that it wouldn't become light where it ran.

Next Sindri threw a lump of gold into the fire. As soon as he turned to work, the fly came back. It settled on Brokk's neck and bit twice as hard as before. The dwarf howled in pain but kept working until Sindri had finished a beautiful arm ring. It was made so cunningly that every ninth night, eight rings as heavy as itself would drop from it.

"Now I am going to make the greatest treasure of all," Sindri said, and threw a lump of iron into the fire. "Do not let the bellows rest for even a second, for this is the gift that will win us the bet."

As soon as Sindri bent over his work, the fly returned. This time it settled between Brokk's eyes and bit so hard that he started bleeding. When Brokk kept pumping, the fly moved to his eyelid and bit till the lid swelled shut. Brokk tried to keep the bellows steady, but when the fly moved to his other eye, he had to let go for just a moment to swipe at the fly and clear the blood out of his eyes.

"Sindri, help!" he yelled, for despite his efforts the fire died down a little. Sindri looked up and moaned, "What have you done?" But when he examined the forge he declared, "The gift has a flaw, but I think it will do."

Out of the forge came a mighty hammer with a head that glowed like fire. "This is Mjolnir the Thunderbolt. With this hammer, Thor will be unbeatable," said Sindri. "Now let us bring these gifts to the gods and see if they don't judge them as the greatest."

Returning to Asgard, Brokk and Sindri handed the gifts over to the gods. Frey, chief of the lesser gods, received the boar and Odin the arm ring. When they handed Mjolnir the Thunderbolt to Thor, Sindri said, "With this hammer you can strike as hard as you like, Thor. It will never break. Whatever you throw the hammer at, you will hit and crush. And no matter how far you throw it, the hammer will turn around of its own and come back to you. Best of all, it can make itself so small that you can carry it on your chest. It has, however, one flaw. The handle is a little short. But," he added, "I made this iron mitten to help you get a good grip."

When the gods saw Mjolnir, they immediately voted it the best gift.

"Brokk is the winner," Odin declared. "Mjolnir is the greatest gift of all, for it will keep us safe. Loki has lost the bet and he must pay with his head."

Grinning wickedly, Loki stepped forward. "Very well. Cut off my head, Brokk. I wagered it. But since my head is attached by the neck and I never wagered my neck, how are you going to get it?"

All went silent. Then Odin spoke. "Loki is right, Brokk. You bargained for his head only, not his neck."

Brokk was furious to be tricked. Still, Loki did not escape unpunished. Brokk was allowed to sew up his lips with a leather thread to stop him from boasting — and the thread did not come off for three months.

Then Brokk and his brother departed for Svartheim, leaving their great treasures in Asgard. And that's how Thor received his mighty hammer, Mjolnir the Thunderbolt.

Tjalvi and the Billy Goats

One day when Thor was racing across the sky with Toothgrinder and Toothgnasher, he decided to spend the night in Midgard and asked for shelter at a farm.

"Come in," said the farmer when Thor asked for a place to sleep. The farmer and his family stared awestruck at the great god with the fiery red hair and bristling beard.

"We haven't much food to offer," apologized the farmer, for he was very poor and could scarcely feed his wife and three children.

"Never mind," said Thor and, without hesitating, slaughtered Toothgrinder and Toothgnasher! Placing the goatskins to one side, he roasted the meat over the fire, paying no attention to the worried looks of the farmer and his family. They certainly didn't want Thor killing his goats just to feed them.

"Eat as much as you like," said Thor when the food was ready. "I ask only one thing. Be careful not to crack any bones. Just return them all to the goatskins."

The family shared a delicious meal with Thor, in spite of knowing they were eating his goats. All followed Thor's instructions except the son of the house, Tjalvi, who loved chewing on meat bones. He gnawed happily away and then, when nobody was looking, carefully broke open one of the bones so he could suck out the marrow inside—his favorite part. Then, without anyone seeing, he returned the broken bone to the goatskin.

The next morning, Thor carefully gathered the bones onto the middle of the skins and waved his hammer over them. Instantly Toothgnasher and Toothgrinder sprang up and started dancing around as though nothing had ever happened—except that Gnasher was limping.

Thor was furious. "Who has done this to my goat? Is this how you repay my generosity?" he bellowed, and swung his hammer. Terrified, the farmer, his wife, and children cowered in the corner, especially Tjalvi, who now, much too late, realized the harm he had done.

Trembling, he stepped forward and whispered, "I am so sorry, Thor. It is my fault. I didn't realize what I did. Please don't punish my family for my wrongs. Punish me instead. Or better yet, let me repay you."

Thor eyed Tjalvi, a scrawny lad of about twelve. "What can a boy like you do for me?" he roared.

"I could be your servant," offered Tjalvi. "I may be skinny, but I am the fastest runner in all of Midgard. I'll run errands for you and work hard."

Scratching his beard, Thor gave Tjalvi's offer some thought. Tjalvi didn't look as though he'd make much of a servant, but Thor never could stay angry for long, and he saw how unfair it would be to punish the whole family for what the boy had done. Finally he agreed. "But you have to promise me this: stay away from my goats."

"I promise," said Tjalvi happily. He hugged his parents and left with Thor in the billy goat cart. From then on Tjalvi was Thor's faithful servant, and the only human ever to live among the gods in Asgard.

A Duel

din was usually wise, but once when he was out exercising his eight-legged horse, he foolishly challenged a jotun named Rugnir to a horse race. They sped across Midgard, all the way to the citadel of the gods. When Odin realized he had allowed a jotun into Asgard, he was very upset, especially since Thor was away. But the laws of hospitality must be obeyed, and Odin invited the giant inside. All the gods were seated at the long table and the only place available was Thor's chair, so Rugnir sat down there and was offered food and drink from Thor's plate and drinking horn. That honor made him so full of himself that he began to boast.

"You may think Thor is strong," he said. "But I am stronger yet. If I wanted to, I could take this entire hall and move it to my country. I could clear out all of Asgard if I wanted, and kill the gods. I would keep only Sif and Freya alive, for I want them for my wives."

Then he called to Freya, the goddess of love and beauty. "Freya, come here and pour me some mead and sit in my lap for a while."

This was too much for the gods.

"Would that Thor was here," Odin said. In that instant, Thor appeared in the doorway, his hammer flashing.

"What are you doing in my seat, drinking out of my horn? Get out this minute so I can finish you off outside," roared Thor. "How dare you enter Asgard!"

"It was your father who let me in," replied Rugnir. "And you'll be counted a coward if you kill me here, for I have none of my weapons with me. Meet me tomorrow at the glaciers in my country and I'll beat you in a duel."

"I'll be there," shouted Thor, and off stormed the giant.

When Rugnir arrived home and told the other giants that he had single-handedly terrified all the gods and would duel Thor tomorrow, they listened eagerly. If they killed Thor, they could overthrow Asgard, and then Midgard would be theirs to plunder.

Rugnir decided his best weapon would be a whetstone, for this kind of stone is used to sharpen knives, axes, and swords; it might therefore be stronger than Thor's Mjolnir. He also decided to use his shield, which was wide and thick and made of granite.

He stood with his shield before him and the whetstone raised and ready for Thor when Tjalvi, running ahead of Thor, arrived.

"Don't hold your shield up high like that, Rugnir," Tjalvi shouted. "Thor is digging a tunnel and will attack you from below."

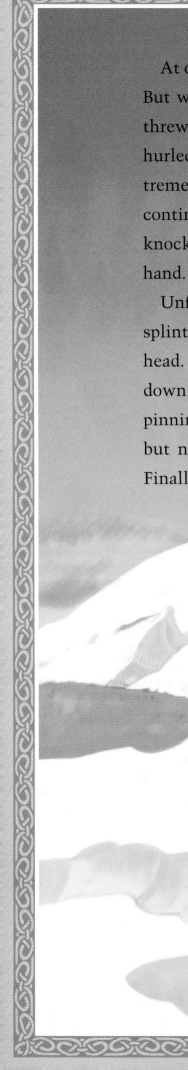

At once Rugnir put his shield down and stood on it for protection. But when Thor appeared, it was not from below! Quickly, Rugnir threw his whetstone as hard as he could. In that same instant, Thor hurled his hammer. The two weapons met in midair. With a tremendous crack and a thunderbolt, Mjolnir broke the whetstone, continued through the air, and hit Rugnir square in the head, knocking him out for good. Then Mjolnir sailed back to Thor's hand.

Unfortunately, when Mjolnir broke the whetstone, that stone splintered off in all directions, and one huge chunk hit Thor in the head. It knocked him over just as Rugnir the giant came crashing down. One of Rugnir's legs landed on top of Thor's neck and back, pinning him to the ground. Hurrying over, Tjalvi lifted and pulled, but no matter how hard he tried, he could not lift Rugnir's leg. Finally Thor shouted, "Run to Asgard for help!"

Tjalvi ran like the wind to fetch the gods, but not one of them was strong enough. Even Odin could not lift the giant's leg. They were scratching their heads and wondering what to do when Thor's little son, Magne, arrived. He was just three years old and his legs were still very short. That's why he hadn't arrived with the other gods.

"I'm sorry I didn't get here sooner, Father," shouted Magne. "I came as fast as I could." He ran over, grabbed Rugnir's leg, and, just like that, threw it off Thor's neck.

"Oh, Father. I bet I could have killed this giant all by myself," said little Magne.

"You know what?" said Thor, "I think you're right. You are a powerful little fellow and I'm proud to call you my son. And because you have saved your father, I'm going to give you Rugnir's horse. Now you can horse-race your grandfather."

"I'd better get home to practice," said Odin, winking his one eye at Magne. Rejoicing, the gods returned to Asgard, Magne riding high on his father's shoulders. This time, he was as much of a hero as Thor.

Outwitted

The biggest and smartest of all the giants was Outgardloki. He had been sending raiding parties into Midgard right under the noses of the gods and not once had they managed to catch them. Thor knew he had to take on Outgardloki and made up his mind to go to the fortress called Outgard, where the giant lived. He decided to bring Loki, for he thought he might need Loki's quick wits. Sometimes, Thor knew, being strong is not enough. Naturally Tjalvi came along, too.

All three jumped into the billy goat cart and took off across the sky. Toothgnasher was still limping, but it didn't slow him down. At nightfall they reached the edge of Jotunheim, the land of the giants. While searching for a place to spend the night, they came upon an empty but odd-looking cottage. There was no front wall, just a gigantic entryway. There were no windows and only one large room, with a smaller one off to the side. Too tired to wonder at the cottage, they went straight inside to sleep.

In the middle of the night, the earth began to heave and bounce like waves beneath them. The cottage trembled and the air filled with a deafening roar. "Run into the side room and hide!" shouted Thor to Loki and Tjalvi. "I will take care of this." Then he tightened his belt, grabbed his hammer, and went to the doorway, ready to fight off any attackers. But nobody came. Thor waited and waited, listening to the roaring, growling, and snorting all night long.

At daybreak Thor, Loki and Tjalvi went outside to see what was making such a racket. And there, next to the cottage, slept the largest giant any of them had ever seen. It was his footsteps that had felt like an earthquake, and his snoring that had kept them up all night.

They looked around and now saw why the cottage was so oddly shaped. It wasn't a cottage at all, but the giant's mitten! The little side room where Loki and Tjalvi had hidden was the thumb.

While they were staring at the huge mitten, the giant woke up.

"What's your name?" asked Thor, not the least bit afraid.

"I'm Skrymir," answered the giant. "And you must be Thor. You're smaller than I expected," he added. "But maybe you're stronger than you look. Where are you going?"

When Thor told him, Skrymir picked up his mitten and said, "I'm headed that way myself. Shall we walk together?"

Thor agreed, although he was irritated at being called small. He made up his mind to show this giant how strong he really was.

After a noon meal, Skrymir wanted to nap. Again the air filled with deafening roars and growls, and Thor decided to teach the giant a lesson. He grabbed his hammer and whacked Skrymir on the head. Opening his eyelids halfway, Skrymir yawned and said, "Did a leaf fall on my head?" Then he fell right back asleep.

Thor could hardly believe it. He grabbed his hammer with both hands and hit even harder than before. Once more Skrymir half woke up and said, "Did an acorn drop on my head?" and fell back asleep, snoring so loudly that nobody else could catch a wink.

Thor was boiling over with rage. His face turned red, his eyes flashed, and his beard trembled, for he knew the giant was making fun of his strength. Tightening his belt and grabbing his hammer again with both hands, he hit the giant so hard that the hammer sank down to the shaft. Skrymir woke up properly this time, but still he just rubbed his forehead, muttering, "Huh! Must be a branch that hit me in the head. But never mind. Time to get up anyway.

"Well, Thor," Skrymir continued. "I guess I'll be on my way. We must part here, for I am going north. Take care. I may be big, but the giants in Outgard are even bigger than I am."

When the billy goat cart arrived at Outgard, Thor, Loki, and Tjalvi were amazed at the size of the castle. The walls were so tall that the travelers had to bend their necks all the way back to see the top. Luckily, the bars of the locked gate were widely spaced, allowing them to climb through.

They walked inside to a hall filled with giants eating and drawling away in their rumbly voices. If the giants saw the intruders, they didn't let on.

Thor strode up to the king, Outgardloki. He was so huge that standing next to him Thor looked like a miniature child. But Thor wasn't afraid. Placing his hand on his hammer, he tipped his head in greeting and said, "Hello!"

The king of the giants kept eating, barely nodding his head in return. What an insult! Thor was furious, for he wasn't used to being received in this way.

Finally Outgardloki announced, "And this little fellow here must be Thor, who we hear so much about. I certainly hope you are stronger than you look, Thor."

Thor glared at him, flexing his muscles and twirling his hammer, but the giant, seemingly unconcerned, asked, "What sports are you and your companions good at? None may enter here without superior skill in some sport."

Loki quickly stepped forward. He was almost as irritated as Thor at their rude reception. "I know a sport I'm reckoned better at than most. I bet none in this hall can eat as fast as I can."

"That's a sport if you're skilled at it," conceded the giant. "And we'll test it."

He called a giant named Burnir and placed a huge trough filled to

the brim with roasted meat in front of them. Loki stood at one end and Burnir at the other.

"READY, SET, EAT!" shouted Outgardloki, and the two, god and giant, fell on the meat. They ate and ate until their faces met in the middle of the trough. Loki had eaten every scrap of meat on his side, but Burnir had eaten the meat, the bones, *and* his half of the trough! Everyone agreed that Loki had lost.

Turning to Tjalvi, Outgardloki asked, "And what is this young fellow good at?"

"I can run faster than anyone," Tjalvi said confidently.

"That's a good sport," agreed Outgardloki, and called a rather small giant lad named Thinkur.

Tjalvi and Thinkur went outside, took their places, and set off.

Tjalvi ran faster than he had ever run before, but still he was only halfway there when Thinkur reached the goal.

"You run fast," grunted Outgardloki, "but not fast enough."

Then he turned to Thor. "Well, Thor. What kind of sport are you good at?"

"Drinking," said Thor at once.

Outgardloki nodded and brought forth a drinking horn. It was unusually large. Still, Thor wasn't worried. He'd drunk with giants before and none had beaten him.

"Some here empty this horn in one gulp," said Outgardloki, "some in two, and there isn't one among us who hasn't finished it off in three gulps."

Glaring at the giant, Thor grabbed the horn, lifted it to his mouth, and drank. When he felt sure he had reached the bottom, he set the horn down. But looking inside, he found to his amazement that it was as though he had hardly drunk at all. Again he lifted the horn and swallowed an enormous gulp. Still there was almost no change in the level inside. Now Thor was really mad. He grabbed the horn with both hands and drank and drank and drank till he could swallow no more. This time the mead had sunk a little, but the horn was nowhere near empty.

Thor was fuming, especially when Outgardloki said, "That is not so impressive, and after all the stories we have heard of you, Thor! Is there something else you can do?"

"What do you want?" roared Thor. His beard trembled with fury and his eyes flashed, for he hated being made fun of.

"The boys here make sport lifting up my cat," said Outgardloki, nodding toward a large black cat that leaped out from a corner.

"What a joke," thought Thor, and placed his hand under the cat's stomach and lifted. But the cat just arched its back and stretched its legs. The more Thor lifted, the more the cat arched and stretched, lifting only one paw off the ground despite Thor's efforts.

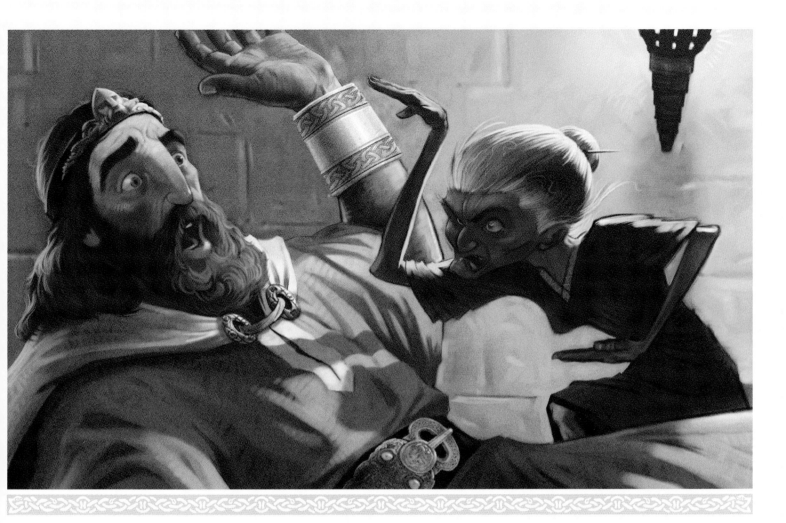

"That's no good, Thor," interrupted Outgardloki. "Maybe you're better at wrestling. He called an old woman. "This is Elle. A lot of the younger boys like wrestling with her."

"I will not wrestle an old woman!" exclaimed Thor in disgust as an ancient woman hobbled next to him. "There's no honor in that." But before he could say another word, Old Elle seized him by the waist and flung him down. That got Thor ready to fight! He grabbed Old Elle and started to wrestle. Holding her in his hands, he tried to bring her down, but she just squeezed him hard and tripped him so he ended up with one knee on the ground.

The giants laughed loudly and their chief shouted, "Thor, you're no match for the giants in Outgard no matter what they say about you in Asgard. But be a sport and eat with us anyway."

Thor was mortified and angry. But he was also hungry, so he ate with the giants. When the meal was over, Outgardloki escorted Thor and his companions out of the hall.

"I guess you don't think much of me," said Thor, embarrassed.

"Now that we are out of earshot of the other giants, I'll tell you the real truth, Thor," said Outgardloki. "I was disguised as Skrymir, the giant you met. When I realized you were coming to Outgard, I knew only magic could protect us. You thought you hit my head with your hammer? It wasn't me, but those hills over there you hit. See those clefts in the mountains? They are from your hammer.

"I had to use several spells to trick all of you," he continued. "Loki, you lost to Burnir because Burnir isn't a giant as you thought. He is really wildfire, and who can consume more than he can? Tjalvi ran against Thinkur, who was actually my thoughts. Nobody can catch up with a thought no matter how fast he runs. And the horn you drank of, Thor? The other end of it dips into the ocean. We were all alarmed when we saw how much you could swallow. You'll see what a low tide you have caused when you reach the sea. The cat you fought is really the Midgard Serpent, the sea serpent that wraps itself around the earth. You had us all in a fright when we saw you lift her. And Old Elle, the old woman you fought so hard, is Old Age. She throws down every man, giant, or god if he lives long enough."

Turning around, Skrymir added, "We fooled you this time, Thor, but from now on, I shall think of even better ways to protect my castle." With that, he disappeared.

Thor hated being tricked. He swung his mighty hammer to destroy the castle of Outgard, but it had vanished.

As Thor, Loki, and Tjalvi traveled home along the seashore, they could indeed see how low the tide had become. Still, they kept silent about their exploits when they returned to Asgard.

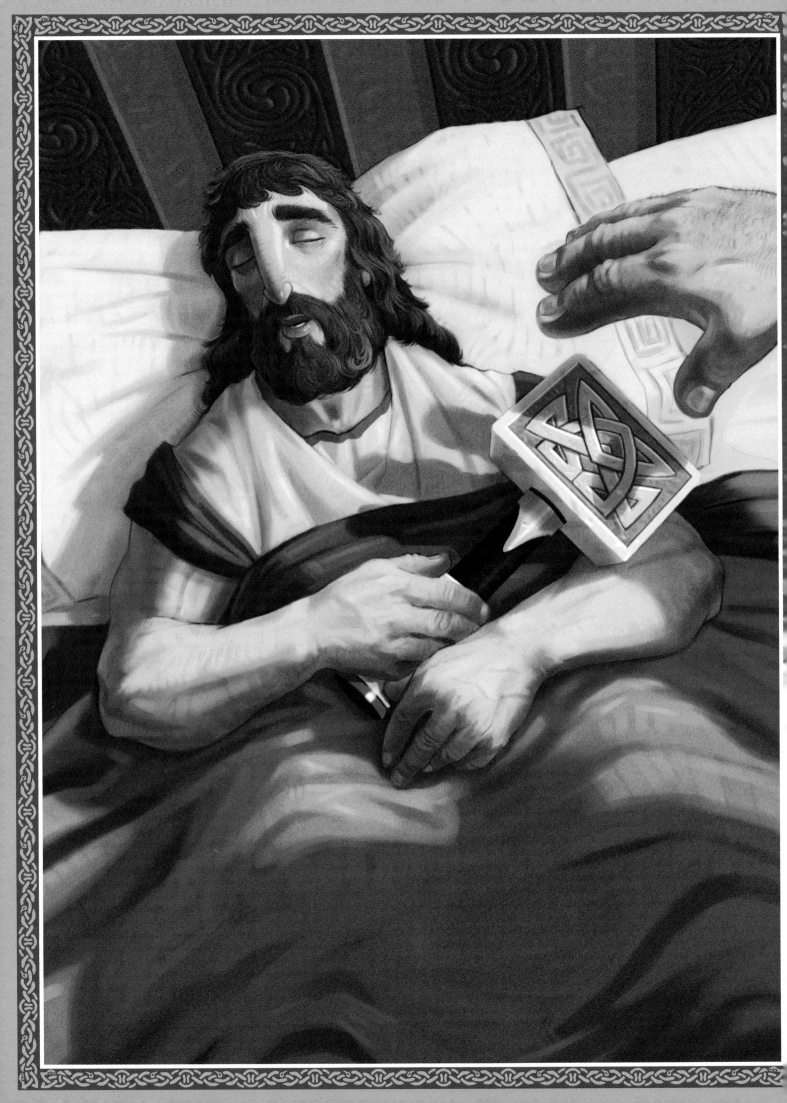

Stolen Thunder

As you can imagine, the giants were always keen to destroy Thor's hammer. But Thor kept his hammer with him at all times, even when he went to bed at night. The trouble was, when Thor was really tired, he slept so soundly that nothing woke him. One morning, after an especially sound night of sleep, the hammer was gone!

"LOKI! LOKI!" roared Thor and charged out of his house. "Where is my hammer?" He stormed into Loki's house and grabbed him by the throat.

"The hammer is gone?" gulped Loki, and turned so pale that Thor realized he was innocent this time. Someone from outside Asgard must have stolen it.

Understanding the terrible danger this put all of Asgard in, Loki quickly said, "Ask Freya for her falcon suit and I'll fly to Jotunheim and look for the thief."

Freya, the goddess of love and beauty, owned a marvelous falcon suit that allowed the wearer to travel at incredible speed. When she heard the news, she too turned white with fear. "Take my suit and find the hammer before the giants hear of this. There is not a moment to be lost."

Loki took off so fast that the falcon wings whistled in the air. He flew across Midgard and into Jotunheim looking for anything suspicious.

After a while he spotted a giant named Trym. Trym was a small but exceedingly rich and greedy giant, and right now he was sitting outside plaiting gold leashes for his dogs and trimming the manes of his horses. He looked smug and pleased with himself. When he saw Loki land near him, he snickered and said, "Well, well, well, if it isn't Loki. And how are the gods today?"

"Not so well," Loki admitted.

"Why would that be?" asked Trym with a smirk.

Looking carefully at him, Loki asked, "Are you the one who stole Thor's hammer?"

"Yes!" Trym blurted out triumphantly. "What's more, I have hidden it eight miles underground and no one will be able to get it, unless..."

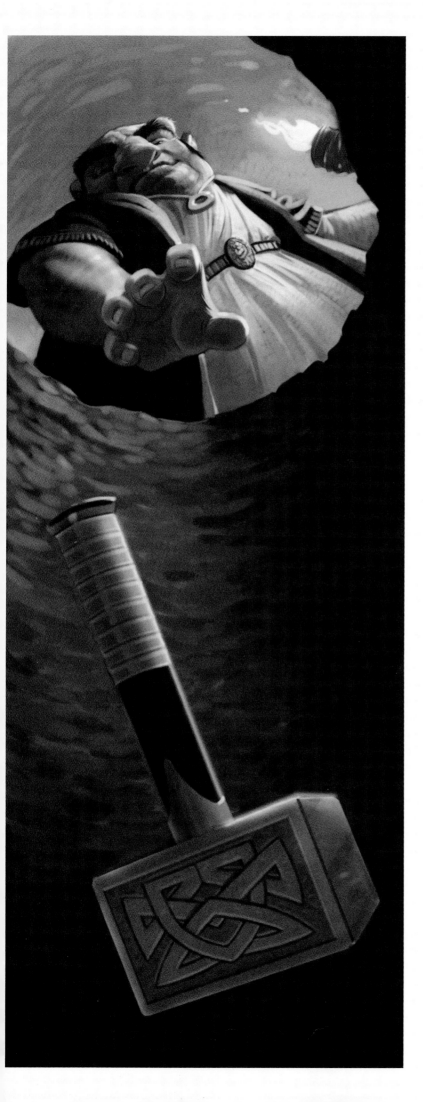

"Unless what?" cried Loki.

"Unless Freya becomes my bride. I will give the hammer to her as a wedding vow!" said Trym.

Loki was horrified at such a demand but promised to pass on the message. He flew back to Asgard as fast as he could.

As soon as Loki had finished his tale, Thor said, "I don't know what Freya will say, but we must ask her."

"Never!" shouted Freya with such energy and fury that her whole house shook and her necklace burst. "Never let it be said of Freya that she was so lovesick she took a giant for a husband."

Now they were in trouble. How could they get the hammer back if Freya refused to marry Trym? All the gods and goddesses were called into council and everyone agreed: Thor's hammer must be  found. But everyone also agreed that Freya should never be made to marry a jotun. What could be done? They debated for days and days. Finally, Heimdall, the god who guarded the rainbow bridge, had an idea. "The only thing that will satisfy Trym is Freya. That is unacceptable, of course," he said, "so Thor, you must go *yourself* dressed up as Freya."

Now it was Thor's turn to roar. "Never!" His red beard shook and his eyes blazed. "I will never dress up as a woman." But he roared in vain.

"You must do it, Thor," said Loki, "or the giants will take over Asgard. Then Midgard will fall next. I will come with you disguised as your maid." Finally Thor agreed.

At once the goddesses took Thor into their chambers and set

about clothing him. They put a lovely long skirt over his hairy legs, dressed him in a pretty blouse, and covered his chest with Freya's sparkling necklaces. A belt with Freya's keys went around his waist. To hide his face and red beard, they tied his hair in a topknot and covered his head with a bridal veil. Then Loki was made up in the same fashion. They made a fine pair indeed!

Tjalvi fetched Toothgnasher and Toothgrinder, and off went Thor and Loki, with such speed that entire mountains burst. Trym heard them coming and shouted to his giant servants and relatives, "Up, up, jotuns. Lay straw on the benches and prepare my wedding feast. I have cattle with horns of gold and enormous treasure. I lacked only Freya and now she is coming to be mine."

By evening the party had assembled for the feast. Thor, as usual, had a good appetite. First he ate all the sweets and delicacies set aside for the women. But that wasn't enough, so he ate an entire roasted steer, and eight salmon, and finished the meal with three barrels of mead.

Trym stared at his bride and exclaimed, "I have never seen a woman take such huge bites and have such an enormous appetite!"

Quickly Loki said, "Oh, Trym. When Freya heard she was to marry you she became so excited she couldn't eat. She hasn't had a bite for eight days because she was pining away for you."

Hearing this, Trym wanted to kiss his bride. He leaned over and pulled the veil aside. But when he saw his bride's eyes he was so startled that he dropped the veil, exclaiming, "Why do my bride's eyes glow like burning coals?"

"That is because she has not slept for eight nights, longing for you," said Loki, the quick-witted maid.

Now Trym became so eager that he commanded, "Bring up Thor's hammer so we can proceed with the wedding and say our vows."

Trym's sister fetched the hammer and placed it in Thor's lap. As soon as Thor felt his beloved hammer, he laughed. He grabbed the handle, tossed off his bridal veil, and flung the hammer with all his might at Trym and the jotuns. *BOOM!* The mighty thunderbolt finished them all off.

Even though Thor was still wearing skirts when he returned to Asgard, nobody teased him, so great was the gods' relief at having Thor and his mighty hammer safely back. To celebrate, they feasted for three days and three nights. Music and laughter rang out from the thirteen mighty halls and reached all the way down to Midgard — where it caused the birds to trill and people to hum and smile for a reason they didn't know at all.

 The End

Glossary and Pronunciation Guide

Asgard (*ahs-gard*). Home of the gods. In the center of Asgard was a beautiful open field called Ida. Surrounding the field were the thirteen halls of the gods. All of Asgard was protected by a huge wall, and it was connected to Midgard with a rainbow bridge.

Brokk (*brock*). A dwarf who made a bet with Loki.

Burnir (*burn-eer*). Wildfire in the form of a giant.

Elle (*ell-ee*). Old Age in the form of an ancient giant woman.

Freya (*fray-ah*). The goddess of beauty and love.

Heimdall (*hame-dahl*). The watchman of the gods. He stands guard at the top of the rainbow bridge that connects Asgard with Midgard.

Jotunheim (*yoh-tun-hame*). The land of the giants. Some sources say it is far to the east in Midgard, separated from it by a huge protective wall. Other sources say it is on the other side of the big sea that surrounds Midgard.

Jotuns (*yoh-tuns*). Giants that have existed since the beginning of time. They are the enemies of both gods and humans. They know magic and can change shape.

Loki (*loh-key*). Odin's jotun foster brother. He is sly, full of mischief, and causes a great deal of harm as well as good.

Magne (*mahg-nee*). Thor's son.

Midgard (*mid-gahrd*). The earth and home to humans, also called Middle Earth.

Midgard Serpent (*mid-gahrd ser-pent*). An enormous serpent that lives at the bottom of the ocean. Its body encircles the earth. A relative of the jotuns.

Mjolnir (*miohl-neer*). Thor's magic hammer, also known as "the thunderbolt." It crushes whatever it hits and always flies back to Thor's hand.

Odin (*Oh-din*). The king of the gods and Thor's father. He is the wisest of all, very old and tall. He has a long beard and only one eye because he sacrificed his other eye to gain wisdom. He is the god of war, and the Vikings called war "Odin's game." A sword was called "Odin's fire." All those who died on the battlefield were received by Odin in Valhall, one of the halls of Asgard.

Outgard (*out-gahrd*). A fortress in the land of the giants.

Outgardloki (*out-gahrd loh-key*). A jotun who was the chief of the giants living in the fortress called Outgard. He disguised himself under the name Skrymir, and was the slyest of the jotuns.

Rugnir (*roog-neer*). A jotun who challenged Thor to a duel.

Sif (*seef*). Thor's wife. She was the goddess of household and family ties.

Sindri (*sin-dree*). The dwarf who made Odin's arm ring, Frey's golden boar, and Thor's hammer.

Skrymir (*skree-meer*). The name that Outgardloki used when he disguised himself to trick Thor.

Sons of Ivald (*sons of ee-vahld*). Two dwarfs who made Sif's new hair, Skipbladnir the ship, and Gugne the spear.

Svartheim (*svahrt-hame*). The home of the dwarfs, located in the northern part of Midgard.

Thinkur (*think-er*). Thought in the form of a giant that Tjalvi had to race.

Tjalvi (*chal-vee*). Thor's servant and the fastest of runners.

Trolls (*trawls*). Members of the giant race. Some of them have many heads. All are huge, ugly, and dangerous. However, they are not very intelligent and they loathe sunshine, which turns them into stone.

Trym (*trim*). A jotun who stole Thor's hammer.

References

It has been said that nobody has a memory long enough to be able to tell all of Thor's wonderful adventures, and these are only some of the tales I know — for whenever the thunder boomed my father used the opportunity to tell me of Thor's amazing exploits. The stories in the collection have been shaped by my childhood memories, readings in Norse mythology, and, of course, by my experiences of telling these tales to American children.

Bækstad, Anders. *Nordiske Guder og Helter (Nordic Gods and Heroes).* Oslo: H. Aschehoug, 2002.

Branston, Brian. *Gods of the North.* New York: Thames and Hudson, 1980.

Crossley-Holland, Kevin. *The Norse Myths.* New York: Pantheon Books, 1980.

Davidson, H. R. Ellis. *Scandinavian Mythology.* London: Hamlyn Publishing Group, 1969.

Hamilton, Edith. *Mythology.* Boston: Little, Brown, 1942.

Storm, Gustav. *Norges Kongesagaer (Sagas of the Norwegian Kings).* Vols. 1–3. Kristiania: J. M. Stenersen, 1899.

Taylor, Paul B. and W. H. Auden. *The Elder Edda: A Selection.* London: Faber and Faber, 1973.

Related Reading

Branston, Brian. *Gods and Heroes from Viking Mythology.* New York: Schocken Books, 1982.

Colum, Padraic. *The Children of Odin: The Book of Northern Myths.* New York: MacMillan Company, 1920.

D'Aulaire, Ingri, and Edgar Parin D'Aulaire. *D'Aulaires' Norse Gods and Giants.* New York: Doubleday, 1967.

Fisher, Leonard Everett. *Gods and Goddesses of the Ancient Norse.* New York: Holiday House, 2001.

Green, Jen. *Gods and Goddesses in the Daily Life of the Vikings.* Columbus, Ohio: Peter Bedrick Books, 2003.

Osborne, Mary Pope. *Favorite Norse Myths.* New York: Scholastic, 1996.